A Cassava Republic Press edition.
First published in the USA in 2018.
First reprint 2019.

First published in Belgium by De Eenhoorn
© Text and illustration: Mylo Freeman

Original Title: Prinses gaat naar School
Copyright 2008 by Uitgeverij De Eenhoorn, Vlasstraat 17, B-8710 Wielsbeke (Belgium)

English Translation copyright © Laura Watkinson, 2017

ISBN 9781911115656

A CIP catalogue record for this book is available from the British Library.

Printed and bound in the UK by Bell & Bain Ltd.

www.cassavarepublic.biz

MYLO FREEMAN

Princess Arabella

Goes to School

CASSAVA REPUBLIC

"It's time to go to sleep now,
sweetheart," said the Queen.
But Princess Arabella couldn't sleep.
Tomorrow's a big day, she thought.
I'm finally going to school!

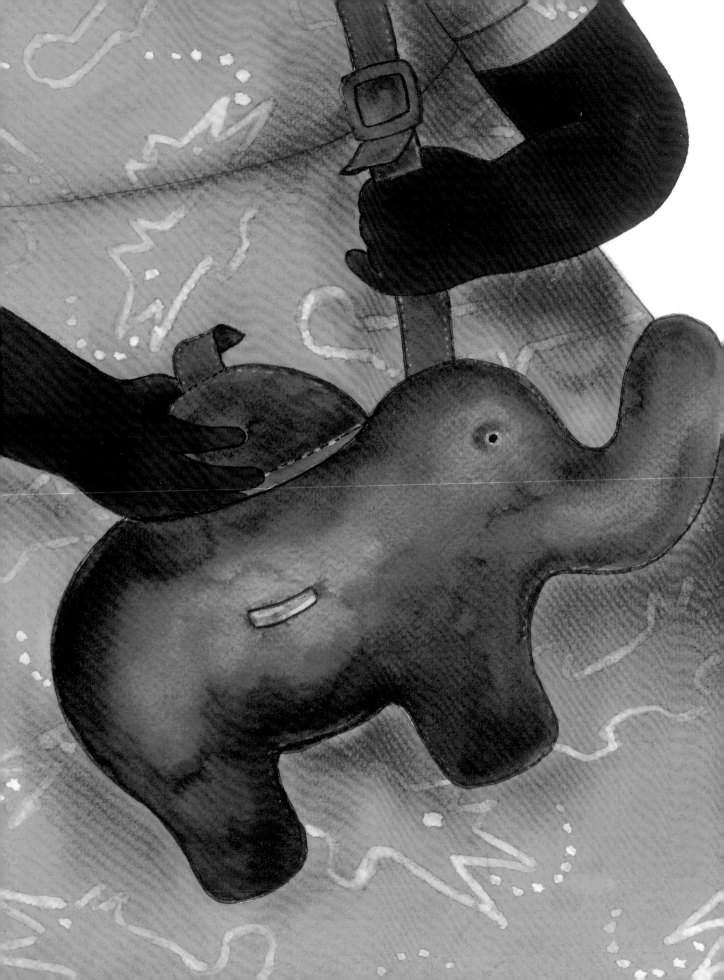

The next morning, Princess Arabella packed her bag for school. Two golden pens, two pencils, an eraser, three books, a golden pencil sharpener and, last but not least, her royal lunchbox.

"You will be good, won't you?" said the Queen.
"You will listen to your teacher, won't you?" said the King.

But Princess Arabella didn't hear a word they said.
She ran into the school as fast as she could.

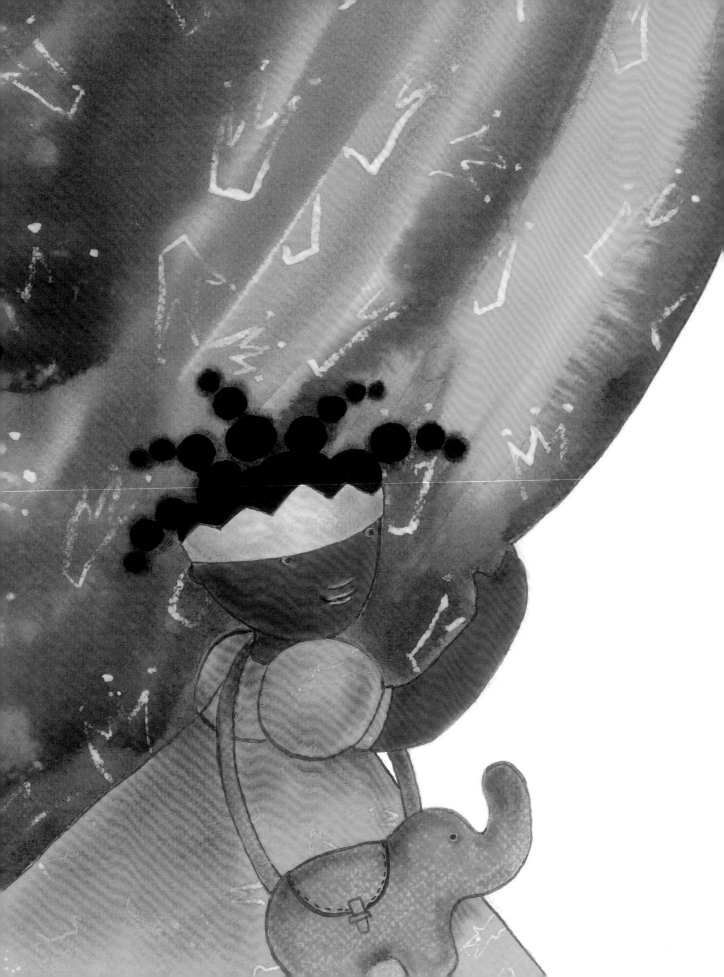

In the classroom, lots of little princesses were bending
and bobbing up and down.
It looks like the gym class has already started, thought
Princess Arabella.

But it wasn't the gym class at all. It was the "How to
Curtsey with Elegance" lesson. And then it was time for
"How to Walk with Grace."
"Noses in the air, girls!" called the royal teacher.
But Princess Arabella thought the book was far too
good to keep on her head.

"Never forget to smile as you cut the ribbon!" called the royal teacher. And Princess Arabella did exactly as she was told. Because she'd just cut out a beautiful chain of elephants!

The princesses' next lesson was math.

"Princess Arabella," said the royal teacher. "1 crown plus 1 crown. How many crowns does that make?"

Arabella didn't answer. What a silly question!

"I don't like school anymore!" said the princess, looking sad. "I want to go home." The royal teacher felt a bit sorry for Arabella. "I have an idea," she said. "Let's make tomorrow a special day. Every princess can bring her favorite animal to school with her!"

And that's what happened. Princess Ling brought her most beautiful butterfly to school…

Princess
Sophie
brought her
favorite cat...

And Princess
Arabella?

Princess Arabella took along her favorite little elephant!
The royal teacher was amazed to see the elephant.
But then she sighed. "Ah, yes, of course," she said.
"What could be more fun than having an elephant in the
classroom?"

Princess Arabella put her hand up in the air as high as she could. "I know, Miss! I know!" she shouted happily. "Two elephants!"